good deed rain

Late last night, when we were all in bed,
Mrs. O'Leary lit a lantern in the shed.
When her cow kicked it over,
She winked her eye and said,
There'll be a hot time in the
old town tonight!

The Bellingham Fire Department is actively investigating the source of a strong sulfur-like odor reported in south Bellingham.

—*Bellingham Today*

DO YOU KNOW WHY YOU'RE HERE?

DO YOU KNOW WHY YOU'RE HERE? ©2025
Allen Frost, Good Deed Rain
Bellingham, Washington
ISBN: 979-8-3492-7452-7

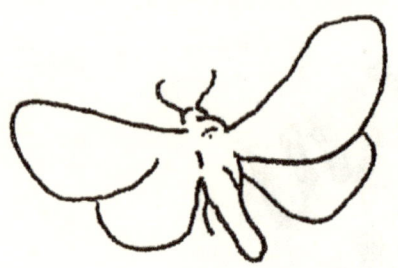

Writing & Drawings: Allen Frost
Cover Photo: Morgan Bush
Cover Production: Robert Millis
Photo of Mabel by Whatcom Humane Society
Quotes:
Folk song "Mrs. O'Leary's Cow"
Bellingham Today, Thursday, August 29, 2024
Bela Lugosi in *Ghosts on the Loose*, 1943
Apple: TFK!

DO YOU KNOW
WHY YOU'RE HERE?

Allen Frost

Good Deed Rain ◊ Bellingham, Washington ◊ 2025

"That was a lucky mistake you made."

—Bela Lugosi

INTRODUCTION

Unbeknownst to me, for two months while I was writing this book, a cow was on the loose around town, avoiding capture. Her name is Mabel and she was spotted here and there, taking the bus, walking through stores, escaping out of doors into the alleys that spider between the buildings. Parks, backyards, overgrown lots, going to movie theaters and flower shops. And she was uncatchable, until October 18. The story of Mabel reminds me of my *Roosevelt* book. That novel features a 1942 elephant seeing the sights. It appears there's an invisible route that animals follow every eighty years or so. When the door opens, they're free to go anywhere they want for a little while.

Also in the air while I'm writing this book, my father has been disappearing before our eyes. A B-movie plot is playing, memories and thoughts have been captured and carried away in specimen jars. A snowy day in Maine in 1950, The Bowery Boys, Basil Rathbone and Charlie Chan, a schoolgirl and crows, his dog Lonzo, California surfboard, family times that circled Seattle, 80 years in between oceans. The tide is carrying a little more every day. This thieving is happening to a lot of people now. Their old age becomes a fog. Is that how it works? That's how it seems to us watching. There doesn't seem to be a way out. Of course that's not true, there is a door in the fog that leads to the next world.

Another thing—every other week this summer, peddlers were knocking on our door. They paid no heed to our gruesome warning sign. Laura bought the sign from some young entrepreneurs who paid us a visit a long time ago. Ironically its purpose was warding off other people like them:

Basil Rathbone

signs were everywhere

I wouldn't say the sign works. Peddlers are fearless. Pied pipers promised an end to ants, mice, rats. We've been targeted by housepainters. Proselytizers with brochures. Arborists. A Lithuanian selling schoolbooks. And yes, a visit from the very roofing crew who start this book. It got me to thinking.

Whatever atmosphere was in the air this fall made for a scary Halloween-time book. The signs were everywhere. After this latest election there's a real feeling that the country has lost its mind. I can't look at a newspaper, I can't watch it unfold anymore. I used to enjoy reading the news, I had a teacher in high school who let us go to his classroom at lunch and read the papers sent to him from around the world. He told me stories of Beirut, when he was a student there, when it was considered the Paris of the Middle East. The buildings were gold with sunlight. He would sit at a café table outside and have mint tea and turn the newspaper pages he was reading. Schoolkids singing, bicycles and taxis. The memory of the sunshine there with olive-colored shadows and birds in the trees overhead.

12/12/24

CHAPTERS

Vampires
19

Nostradamus Investment Corporation
20

Old World
22

New World
25

The Television Thief
31

Remedy
35

Phinneas
39

Ms. Meredith
43

From a Jar of Ponds
46

Double-Feature
48

Two Days Later
50

Reception
52

The Contract
55

Meet Count Misfit
59

The Song
62

Gary Cooper
65

Gold
68

Stars
71

Lexington Brown is Not Around
75

Olson Redding's Book
78

Flowers
80

Sunset Drive
82
Details
84
Halloween
87
Legs O'Toole
91
Lurking
94
Trick-or-Treaters
97
Holler Farm
101
Lantern
105
Hospital
109
An Old Friend
112
Luckily
115

1.

VAMPIRES

There were three of them. The first one stopped by the gate and called, "Hello?" She stared at the house. She knew someone was inside. Silvery light flickered on the window.

Darvis was watching TV. When he looked around the curtain, he saw a girl standing in the driveway.

"Hello?" she called again.

Darvis paused the movie as Ida Lupino was stepping into a black-and-white boat. Her foot was half in the fog. He knew what would happen to her, he saw this movie before. Poor Ida was in trouble.

He opened the screen door and the girl outside was quick to introduce herself.

"And I love the lavender," she added, pointing at the garden round the base of the fir tree. Purple flowers. A boy wandered behind her with a clipboard. They both wore the same red and white shirt uniform. "We're a local business. We noticed your roof."

"My what?" Darvis cupped his ear.

"Sorry." She touched the air. "Are you at all concerned about the moss growing on your roof?"

Darvis told her he could take care of it. He would too—every few years he risked his life going up on the slanted peak to spread a can of Moss-B-Gone. Moss grew on everything like the fog in the movie he was watching.

The girl looked to her right and introduced another co-worker. She said her friend's name, but it didn't matter to Darvis, all he saw was her eyes. They weren't human eyes, they were filled with black ink, they shined like coal. She stuck her hand out towards him.

"I know why you're here," Darvis said and called, "Lincoln!" before anything worse could happen. The air burred as Lincoln bounded past him.

The three vampires in the driveway hissed backwards.

Darvis didn't need to douse them with holy water, their feet scattered the gravel as they ran down the driveway and around the corner rhododendron, clopping the sidewalk. He waited until he couldn't hear them before he called Lincoln to come back inside. 32nd Steet returned to the sound of cars and a crow on the telephone pole.

This was the second time this week the vampires had been to his house. They were getting daring. They wanted him—it seemed only a matter of time. How long could he hold them off? Time for some fresh garlic along the picket fence. The European Market sold them in big loops.

No—Darvis remembered—this was the third time! First there was the rat-killer on Monday, and after that someone selling encyclopedias. The roofers were third in line. The town must be on a migratory route.

The sidewalk—what he could see of it in front of him—was empty. Safe for now. He turned around and went in the house.

The television glowed in the gloomy room. Ida Lupino was frozen in a nighttime boat. She seemed to realize the danger she was in. For the first time.

2.
NOSTRADAMUS INVESTMENT CORPORATION

"What am I doing with a cricket team? I don't know anything about cricket. The bug maybe, yes, but not the game. I don't know what I was thinking…Yes. Yes, that's right…Thank you, sir…Yes, I'll take the loss. I just want out of the deal."

It's a wonder Nostradamus Investment Corporation stays in business. His premonitions were never right. You'd do better off believing the opposite.

"I'm very grateful." Ewell Clagg hung up the phone and pumped his fist. What a relief! A twelve-grand loss was nothing. He could cover that. He could make a call.

A little story played out as he stared at the window. He always wanted to own a franchise. That's what millionaires did. He was hoping for a basketball team, he wanted a seat on the court. Then he saw a flyer on the 7-Eleven billboard: *Own Your Own Cricket Team.* So he bought one. It didn't take him long to realize he owned the worst cricket team in the league. He had no idea how to turn it around. Until now.

He grinned. If he hadn't sold his deed, imagine what would happen. Well, even then it wouldn't be Ewell's first bankruptcy. Big deal. He laughed as he ripped up the latest copy of *Cricket Digest*. Good riddance, what a relief to be rid of that. He dropped the scraps into the wastebasket.

If only Nostradamus Investment Corporation bore the slightest resemblance to its namesake. In a way, their track record didn't matter. He didn't have to worry about losing money. He had plenty of it. And Ewell was sure that sooner or later, he'd land that mythical cash cow.

He felt better and there was no reason not to. He opened the *Herald* to the comics page. Before he found it, he reached in his pocket for a cigarette. He lit one, started to turn the page and coughed the cigarette out.

A drawing of a cartoon cow with the caption: *Own Your Own Dairy Farm*. He snatched the cigarette off the desktop and got it going again.

This was something that always interested him. He used to tell people in school about his imaginary family. His parents were famous explorers. He had a brother. And he had a pet cow. Eventually he put it out of his mind, but now it returned, and it wasn't a fantasy—it could be real. All he needed was a big backyard. And think of all the dairy products he would get for free. It actually made sense to have a pet cow.

He had that feeling, that lucky feeling, and he reached for the phone again.

the slightest sound

3.

OLD WORLD

Lincoln settled back into his pillow on the couch. The movie was long over. Poor Ida survived. Darvis was asleep. Lincoln kept one eye open, always on the lookout for more vampires. Like science fiction, this is how they survived, while all around them the old world crumbled.

Other people couldn't tell the danger they were in, they just went about their lives until they were over.

Not Darvis. He saw behind the scenes. He had been cursed by Count Misfit. At night when the gate latch rattled, Darvis was sure it was something sinister. It wasn't easy being constantly on alert, it took a toll. Darvis used to wake at the slightest sound. A gnawing at the baseboard, or feet running in the attic.

He was getting better though, he was working on it—he had reason to—her name was Deena. Slowly, he was joining the living.

Lincoln left the couch and stopped beside the window.

Darvis yawned and stretched and opened his eyes. "What is it? We okay?" He sat up and followed Lincoln's gaze. "Look at that poor fellow..." An old man walked very slowly along the street. It seemed as if the sidewalk was a current running against him. A month ago, Darvis would have been sure this was another victim of vampires. It was a rotten idea, but he was seeing people close to him starting to go, almost suddenly, as if something cruel got a hold of them, took their minds away. It was an explanation. A plot right out of a Count Misfit midnight movie, only it wasn't blood the vampires were after, they were stealing memories. They were carting away life stories, leaving their hollowed-out victim on autopilot, floating in a tide controlled by an unseen push. Without memory, you were living on borrowed time. Without memory, who were you?

"Come on," he told Lincoln. "We better help him."

There was always a car coming or going on 32nd Street and often someone on the sidewalk walking a dog or headed to the bus stop or just passing houses the way ghosts do.

Another 1941 movie was on TV. A woman sparkled jewelry. Darvis opened the door and let Lincoln rush outside. Darvis ran his hand along the rail, down the cement steps, careful of the dry blackberry vine. The steps could be daunting. He wasn't that young himself.

He opened the gate where the girl stood last summer, latching it behind him. Lincoln watched through the fence slats as Darvis descended the driveway slant to the sidewalk.

A sparrow darted from the hawthorn, flew in front of Darvis into the blue hydrangea leaves next door. At least it wasn't a bat.

"Hello!" Darvis called.

The old man was just ahead, marching slow as a deep-sea diver. One more ancient step and halt.

"Are you okay?" Darvis asked. "Do you need help getting anywhere?" Since Darvis became aware of the vampire assault—he didn't know how to stop it, he didn't know if he could—he tried his best to help the victims.

The old man turned slowly and said, "You got a car?"

"Sure."

"Then you can drive me to the pharmacy."

4.
NEW WORLD

"Who's your new friend?" Deena asked.

"Oh gee…" Darvis sighed. "That's Thornton. I'm his chauffeur today." He explained to her how his good deed led him to the pharmacy then the post office, the bank, and now the market. Darvis was tired. He'd been on the run since he left home. He leaned on the grocery cart like a man roped to the oar of a Roman galley.

"Here," Deena said and gave him a strawberry from her basket. The taste made him dizzy.

"Ohhh, that's good," he said and shut his eyes. For a moment a new world welcomed him. She was still there when he opened his eyes. "Thank you."

"I'm making strawberry shortcake."

"Oh my God."

She laughed.

He said, "Homemade strawberry shortcake is the greatest thing on Earth."

She laughed again. "Well, you're welcome to stop by

and have some with me." When her hand touched him, he smiled. This feeling was still overwhelming. With the world in such a state, vampires loose and on the hunt, he couldn't believe his luck, he didn't know how this happened, it happened out of the blue, and day by day she was changing the world. When they were together, even the grocery store became the set on a beautiful planet. And there was her house, over the next rise, just follow the strawberries.

He said, "I would like to, I will. I'd cross a desert to be there."

"Darvis, you don't have to do that. You know where I live. There are no deserts in sight." Then she pointed down the aisle, "Here comes your friend."

Thornton crawled towards them at a snail's pace. He was clutching a box of raisin bran.

Darvis groaned. "How did I get myself into this? All I want is to run off with you and your strawberries." He let go of the grocery cart, eyes bright, "Come on! Let's go! There's still time before he gets here!"

"Darvis, you can't leave him stranded."

"Yes I can! He's superhuman, I didn't realize until I got roped in. He never gets tired."

She cocked her head. "You drove him here, Darvis. You better bring him back. But don't worry..." she took a step away, "The greatest thing on Earth will be your reward." She waved. "See you at seven o'clock." Oh, she knew how to talk like an RKO movie.

one Saturday morning

5.
The TELEVISION THIEF

When he was seven or eight, Darvis got caught stealing a television. Perhaps that sounds worse than it was. There were no police involved, no Devil's Island sentence. His mother rented the basement studio to a young couple. Darvis had been down there with her a few times and his eyes were always roaming, noticing this and that but most of all their small black-and-white TV.

One Saturday morning long ago, Darvis was up early in time for his show. He poured a bowl of cereal, added milk, only spilling some of it on his way to the living room. Nobody would find the spill in the shag and the spot would dry once the sun crawled in the window. He set the bowl on the coffee table in front of the couch. The spoon hung over the edge like an oar. But when he clicked the TV on, nothing happened. What was wrong with it? It worked last night when he watched *Rhoda* with his mom. In the time between, something in it died that not even Dr. Frankenstein with all his electricity could fix. Darvis was a smart boy though. He just needed to think of something else. That's how he remembered the television downstairs. He knew exactly where it sat in their room on a shelf along the wall. If Plastic Man was here, he would reach out the window with an arm that kept stretching to the window below. He would raise that and slip his hand through curtains and down some more, his fingers would claw around the TV's handle. Suspenseful music would be playing as he lifted the television and pulled his arm back to Davis in the living room. Plastic Man could do anything. And his cartoon was on in three minutes! Darvis had to act fast.

He ran to the kitchen and opened the cupboard and took a brass key off a hook. The clock said two minutes until Plastic Man, time was ticking. The door was covered with coats that swung and sighed when he opened it. A scarf wanted to come with him but he shook it off. Down the steep steps as quiet and quick as he could, Darvis reached the door below and fit the key. This is the part where Plastic Man would just fold himself and slip under like a letter, but Darvis had to think I'm invisible, I will do this and nobody will know.

He stepped into the basement room peeking around the shield of the door. Some gray daylight came through the window. It was a sleeping room, sure enough they were on the bed on the floor in the corner still asleep. His eyes went to the TV. Plastic Man couldn't wait—in a minute the music would begin and he would be in a new adventure. Twenty feet there, ten seconds to unplug it and coil the wire and heave it to his chest then only twenty feet back to the upstairs door. He nearly made it.

"Hey," said a dreamy voice. "You taking my TV?"

Darvis froze.

The lady on the bed stirred, "What is it?"

"That kid's got our TV."

With a mind sharpened on Warner Brothers cartoons, Darvis slowly turned towards them. His slitted eyes were barely open. He slowly retraced his steps to the shelf where he settled the television, plugged it back in to the wall and turned, his arms held out like a sleepwalker in a movie. Creeping like that, he left the room, shut the door and ran up the steps.

slow-motion circles

6.
REMEDY

These days Darvis thought about Deena. She was even leaning into his dreams. If there were vampires, they were only nightmares. What was the point of holding onto that? Love made you alive. He wished he ran off with her from the grocery store, but no, she was right, he had good deeds to do. Thornton was his responsibility until the moment he drove to an apartment on Clementine Street and let him depart.

The car door shut. Darvis watched Thornton leave with a grocery bag. That old man was no victim of phony vampire peddlers, he ran slow-motion circles around Darvis. Like chasing a bumblebee all around town. It was tiring. Darvis held onto the steering wheel almost without the life to turn the key and get out of there. Thornton carried his groceries up a stairway. His shadow rose along the pebbled wall. Darvis didn't mean to be gone this long. It was afternoon. Where had the day gone?

Then he remembered Lincoln was waiting at home. He remembered Deena. She might be chopping strawberries right now. And he found the energy to start the car.

On the floor by the pedals was a crumpled brochure.

One of peddlers who visited during summer was Ogden Moot. From a safe distance Darvis took the time to listen to Ogden's pitch. He even asked questions. Ogden was selling memory gel. He ran a small local business he said, he and his granddaughter made the batches. He held a jar up to the afternoon sun so Darvis could see the light shining through. It was blue as a tropical ocean. Darvis wondered if it would work. He was worried about a friend, Ms. Meredith. Her memory loss was getting worse. If only she kept copies of her favorite memories on a shelf like those records with songs you couldn't forget. If only it was that easy. She would need a lot more than some huckster's remedy. And how many times was Ogden going to repeat, "When reality is unsticking, there's no substitute for Moot's Memory Relief." He was worse than A.M radio.

Darvis told him no thanks. No potion could stop death creeping in. Sooner or later you have to surrender, but not this way, with your thoughts erasing, forgetting your time here was a brief miracle.

On Aurora, he drove past the stands crowding the sidewalk. Traffic was slow. Stopped at a red light, he saw the flower seller and thought of Deena. The light turned green, he was passing more vendors. They crowded the sidewalk. Smoke was rising from grills, balloons and flags and racks of clothes.

Darvis drove past a magic carpet lot. They were roped in rows like clotheslines. The owner Otto Kott stood in front of one of his carpets, one with a big price taped on: *ONLY $289!* He watched the traffic and waited.

nervously edging along

7.
PHINNEAS

Cars were acting strange on the parkway. They had a cow-like quality, nervously edging along step by step and stopping. Darvis soon found out why. There was a dog walking in the center of the road, right along the yellow line. The traffic stalled, everyone in the herd watched the dog, some rolled down windows, some called from open doors. The dog paid no attention. It trotted in the middle, its flanks were muddy, but Darvis knew who it was.

He steered to the curb and hopped out of his car. "Phinneas!" he called. Holding out his hand to stop the next approaching car, Darvis went into the road. "Phinneas! Come here."

The dog heard his name and hurried towards Darvis. Phinneas looked like he crawled from a haunted tomb, eyes wide, tongue hanging, white and gray fur matted with dirt.

"Come on, Phinneas." Darvis patted the dog's shaggy neck and took hold of the collar and led him to the car. "It's okay, I'll take you home. Don't worry." The dog got in the car and sat on the passenger seat.

All the stalled cars were moving again. As soon as he could merge, Darvis turned at the light on 30th to cross the Arco parking lot, past the gas pumps and he rejoined the parkway. It was about a half mile up the hill to the dog's house. Phinneas had come a long way on his own. And what a state the dog was in. He must have followed the creek and the culvert until it ran into a pipe under the road where he clawed up the embankment to join the traffic.

The road passed beneath the highway and became a new avenue rising steeply up a winding hill. The car climbed it with a groan. Phinneas had calmed. He grinned at the windshield where a few dots of rain landed. Trees and houses.

"I'm glad you found me," Darvis said. "Is that what you were doing—looking for help?"

Like a stream on a mountainside, the road banked right then left, over and over braiding itself until it was there at the top of the hill. Behind the car was the sea and the islands flying gray clouds on kite string.

The car entered a driveway, snapping over gravel. Phinneas was excited now, whining, on his feet.

"Here we are," said Darvis. Ms. Meredith lived in a beautiful old wooden farmhouse set like a crown in a sloping field. Darvis parked beside her car, underneath a big oak tree. Phinneas brushed against him excitedly. The engine gave a cough as it shut off.

"Hang on, Phinneas." The dog had a muddy foot on Darvis who was working to open the door. "Let me get out first." But soon as the door unlatched the hound bumbled over his lap. Darvis stood up, lost sight of the dog around the house. His shoes popped on the fallen acorns.

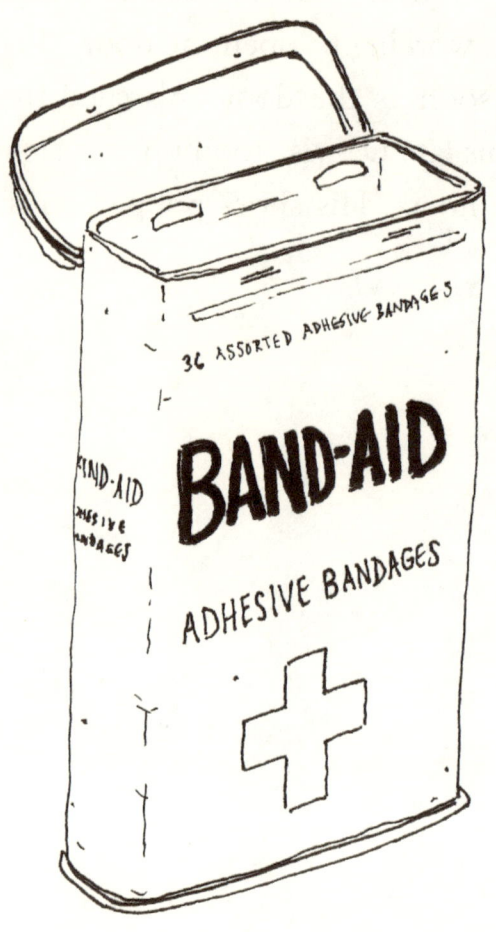

redwing blackbirds

8.
MS. MEREDITH

Phinneas barked ahead of him.

Darvis rounded the corner of the house and he had a view of the hillside, the cropped lawn and the pond.

Phinneas barked again. His bushy tail wagged. He stood over Ms. Meredith. She lay flat in the mud.

Darvis ran towards them. A path between dead asters and deadheaded daisies led to the water. It was the first of October, the summer flowers were gone, the lavender was brown. "Ms. Meredith!"

She lifted an arm too weak to wave. "Darn the luck," she muttered as he reached her. She lay on her back looking into the sky like someone waiting for a hundred redwing blackbirds to raise her up. She was frail, they could probably do it.

"Are you hurt?"

"No dear. I just slipped. That's all."

"Here, can I help you to stand?"

"Oh alright. Move aside Phinneas."

The dog whined but complied.

It was no wonder she slipped. The ground around the pond was slick moss. Darvis got hold of her and pulled her from the water's edge and even with his sore arm—arthritis or something—he was able to lift her upright. She was light, airy as a bird. In a fairytale he could have carried her like a bindle. "Where were you trying to go?"

In a moment, watching her feet, she said, "I forget." Then she seemed to be somewhere else, "How are you?"

They were back on crushed clover, he said, "I'm fine." Darvis explained how Phinneas got help. "He's a courageous dog."

Phinneas was, it's true.

"We should get you to the house. Can you keep going?" Darvis remembered the photo the *Herald* ran—this was years ago—when Ms. Meredith was an archive librarian. That was the day the library was throwing out their card catalogs. These were magnificent nautical-looking cabinets filled with the world's knowledge. The photo in the newspaper showed Ms. Meredith sitting on one, getting carried outside to a truck like a Viking burial pushed to sea.

She said she was fine. "Can you get my cane?"

He did.

Phinneas kept pace with them, close to her as a sail. When they reached the house, Phinneas was first up the porch steps. He pushed the door open with his long, bristled nose.

The cabinet radio played inside. She liked orchestras and quartets. Ms. Meredith said she got distracted. She only went outside to look at the pond. She wanted to see if a blue heron landed.

9.
FROM a JAR of PONDS

Over ten years ago, Lexington Brown delivered the pond. Ms. Meredith waited for him in the field in a hollow below the oak. She had the perfect spot. One foot rested on her shovel beside a freshly dug hole.

Lexington came down the hill in careful slow motion. He carried a jar full of water. She waved at him. He was watching where he put his feet. The grass was a little long and there was still morning dew to soak his shoes. You couldn't see the mountain peaks with the usual rain clouds to hide them, but you knew where they were.

"Hello!" she called.

He didn't answer, he didn't hear her, the machinery of so many inventions made him a little deaf. Once he got closer, when she called him again, that time he heard. He smiled and held up his empty hand. "I brought you something."

She stepped back while he kneeled by the overturned ground.

"Is this where you want the pond?"

She nodded.

He said, "Do you know the story of the Princess and the Pea?"

"Oh yes," she said. "Hans Christian Andersen." She could have said more. A librarian knows books the way a shepherd knows the flock. But she was watching him set the jar down so he could find something in his coat pocket.

He held a diamond-like bead on his open palm. He chuckled. "This is the pea that will make so much commotion." She noticed the way his hand trembled. He let it roll off his hand into the ground.

Lexington took the jar in both hands and unscrewed the lid. More shaking, a little water spilled. "And this is the blanket that goes over it." He poured. It began with just that small pool.

The rain would find it, more water would blanket it, and a well that was hidden underground would reach up and help to fill it more.

That wasn't all. That diamond bead also contained cattails, irises, lily pads, and the white lotus flowers she loved. And as it grew and added all its elements, the pond would call to the birds, dragonflies, frogs and even a turtle would eventually settle in. It seemed like a miracle. Brown had shelves of them. This one came from a jar marked Monet's Pond.

10.

DOUBLE-FEATURE

Signs on doors, closed stores, less cars on the road. Stay at home. Listen to the goodnight birds. A tin can rolls in the street.

Darvis was finally home, on the couch, with Lincoln by his side and another movie on TV. It was early October and Halloween was casting its spell already. On the screen was a haunted house. The camera moved through an eerie fog.

"I wonder what will happen," Darvis said in a voice that wasn't too convincing. He had a pretty good idea what would happen next. Before the girl opened the door, he wanted to warn her it would be better to turn around, go back through the branches and fog to where she left her broke down car. Lock the doors, hide on the backseat, pull that blanket over yourself and be still like someone waiting for a dream to change. Of course he couldn't tell her, that was the point of movies like this, you could watch all the wrong things happen and be glad it wasn't you.

"There she goes," he told Lincoln. Everything was up to her wits from now on. He left her with Lincoln while he brought his empty soup bowl to the kitchen.

It was almost time to see Deena. She would be interested in hearing about Phinneas leading him to Ms. Meredith. It could be a double-feature to the movie playing in the other room. He would tell it like that. Urged down the narrow one-way road off Potter Street where the black-and-white B-movie theater used to be. Take a seat. Watch Darvis rescue a dog off the street and drive it up a creaky avenue to a wooden Gothic house on top the hill. Lightning lights the sky. Watch as the car parks and the dog runs into a moonlit field, to a pond where an old woman's body lies in the mud. See Darvis rescue her, she seems alright, he brings her back to the house. She says she's fine but isn't that what they always say? A night like this, the vampires could be out. If her neck has been bitten, he can't tell. Only he can find where her memories went...a basement in a castle where Count Misfit grows movies that haunt the night.

When Darvis was done washing the dishes, he left them to dry. It was 6:30.

11.
TWO DAYS LATER

Two days later while Darvis was making coffee, the phone rang. He thought it might be Deena, he hoped it would be, and his voice was bright as he answered, "Good morning!"

"Is this Tuesday?"

He recognized the voice, but the question threw him. The names of the days didn't matter so much to him anymore. Now that he didn't have to be at work, time took on a whole new meaning. The sun rose and set, the moon looked in the window while he slept. No, he couldn't remember what day it was exactly, but considering who was asking, he knew Tuesday was just a name.

"This is Darvis, Ms. Meredith. Are you trying to call Tuesday?" Tuesday was the caregiver who went to her house on Mondays.

"Darvis?"

"Yes."

"Where am I?"

"You're at home. You're talking to me on the phone."

Then she said, "There's a cow in the meadow."

At times like this you couldn't be sure if Ms. Meredith was dreaming or slipping into a memory that was just as real as it once had been. She could be a girl again in 1951.

"A cow?" he said. Darvis tried to imagine where she was, standing in the weeds where the gate was left open and a black-and-white cow materialized?

"Yes," she said. "A man from the telephone company brought it here. I don't want it to eat my garden, I have enough trouble with the deer."

"Do you want me to come over?"

"I don't know where Tuesday is."

"Alright Ms. Meredith. Don't worry. I'm on my way. I'll see you soon."

He hung up the phone. Now he was picturing a cow fifty years ago when this town had farmland and forest cover. He saw the cow, that part was easy to imagine, but it was harder to see the girl. Ms. Meredith was always old, wasn't she?

The open coffeemaker sat like an unfinished masterpiece. There were grounds in the filter, but he didn't have time to add water and brew. If a cow was really in the meadow, that was something he wanted to see. If he got there and it was another delusion, he would call Tuesday.

"Come on Lincoln," he said. "Let's go."

12.
RECEPTION

For a long time, she was a regal figure in the library. You knew right away she was someone who knew things. She was Ms. Meredith. She still was, even if she and the library had lost something that made a glow. She was outside by her car with her back turned when Darvis arrived. A hand was on a hip, she was looking down the hill towards the pond, either watching a real cow or the ghost of one. It didn't make sense, but Darvis hoped he was about to see a cow too.

He and Lincoln left their car. The morning was crisp, especially so under the tall oak tree where the leaves had begun to gather and crackled underfoot. Darvis didn't want to surprise her, she still hadn't turned. He made the word Hello sound drawn-out as the foghorn down on the bay.

Her hand moved from her hip and made a curt wave. She knew he was there, she just couldn't look away from what she was watching.

"Hello Ms. Meredith…" His voice trailed off as he saw what was there in the meadow. If it was a dream, they were sharing it. The dream starred a large black-and-white dairy cow.

Darvis said, "How?..." and stopped. You don't see cows in town anymore. Time and technology had erased them from the scene. A half-hour drive into the county, they would start to reappear, a cow would be natural there, where the flats were green and wide enough to hold herds of them. Not here though. It was like seeing a kangaroo.

Ms. Meredith said, "The man brought it."

"What man?"

"The man in the truck. The man from…wherever…"

"Pacific Telephone?"

She looked confused. Darvis was too.

Why would someone from the phone company bring her a cow? Was this a reward for longtime customers, for a life of paying bills on time? Would a cow in your yard improve your reception? Was it a publicity stunt for the new service placing calls to the moon? It was absurd.

It didn't matter. Darvis couldn't take his eyes off the cow either. It existed in this place, at this time like a television cow until someone turned the channel. What did it do? Nothing at the moment. It wasn't wearing roller-skates or swimming laps in the pond. Cows have their own sense of purpose. This one was just fine with this October morning. There were no more dragonflies this late in the season, no clover anymore, at least none that Darvis could see.

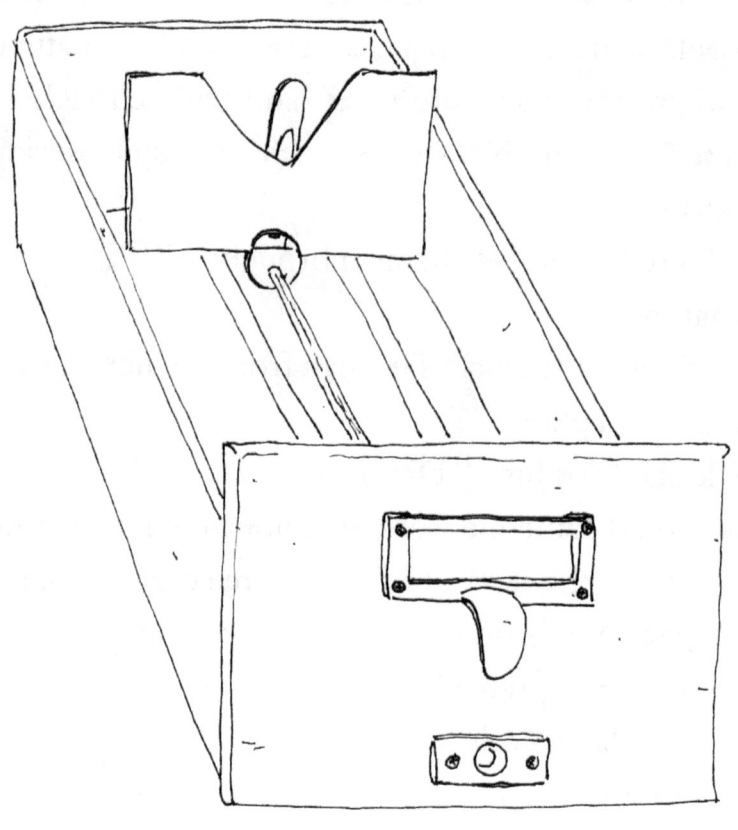

where was the librarian?

13.
The CONTRACT

Ms. Meredith left the paperwork on the kitchen table. The empty coffee cup was where Ewell Clagg sat when he turned the pages and signed the cow over to her trusteeship as equal partners in the venture. "I don't understand any of it," she told Darvis. "Do you?"

He had to fish his glasses out before he could try. "This isn't from the phone company. Is that what he told you?"

"Yes. I think so."

"This part isn't even words, it's just a lot of random typed letters." He flipped the page and read below the signature line, "Ewell Clagg, Nostradamus Investment Corporation." He took a sip from his own cup of coffee. "That's not Pacific Telephone."

She looked far past the table, her blue eyes like a sailor seeing only ocean before forever and ever. Where was the librarian who knew every fine line in a document?

Darvis couldn't look at her this way. He turned his attention to the black coffee in his cup and finished it in a gulp. His finger was caught in the tight curved handle. Who had hands like this, to hold such a dainty thing? Ms. Meredith's glass-faced cupboard was filled with the blue and white china pattern. Fragile things. The contract felt like a bomb wanting to blow everything up.

Darvis said, "There's no address for this guy, no phone number, no contact. He just dropped off a cow and left?"

This was too much for her, Darvis could tell. She had been preyed upon. What sort of monster would do this? Confusion settled on her like a London fog, she was transformed.

Vampires.

Where did he get such an idea about vampires? It wasn't something he came up with—blame it on TV. Blame it on *The Count Misfit Show*.

For a long time, the television was the only other human voice in his house. Movies and detectives kept him company. That wasn't so unusual, lots of people at the end of a long day will sit down and be carried away. Dreams aren't only in us, they surround us. From one dreamworld to another, different but connected. One Friday night, Darvis was watching a black steamship on a gray sea and the people aboard were silver murmuring and when he woke up it was later. Another movie was on. The ship was long gone. A car was driving in the dark. A man and a woman staring at the narrow road. A countryside of black silhouettes, trees shapes, twisting and turning in the headlights. Not far ahead two dim figures moved a hedge across the road. They hung a lantern on it and a Detour sign. The arrow pointed into a lane where the car's engine would freeze in a radio beam and the car would bump to a stop and the two passengers would have to get out. They didn't know they were captured. Their minds were blank. A thousand cricket soundtrack. A distant window light. The hedge moved back where the lane began.

monsters roamed

14.

MEET COUNT MISFIT

When Darvis was ten, he stood in line at Food Giant to meet Count Misfit. He wasn't the only one. He stood behind rain jackets, wool coats and wet sweaters and every moment or so, when he dared, he leaned around to look ahead. Just for a peek. That was all his courage allowed.

Back at home was a black-and-white TV. It was a window that showed a different world, like ours in many ways, but also like a dream, where people could fly and animals could talk and monsters roamed and there was no color. When Darvis saw Count Misfit sitting at a folding card table signing autographs with a record playing scary Halloween sounds, so close, he could barely breathe the same air. He waited all week to be here, ever since he saw the sign taped in the window. *Meet Count Misfit In Person!* Written in dripping blood letters. Each step forward brought him closer to that table and he couldn't look anymore, his courage was fading, he looked at the tan linoleum floor. Footprints marked the tiles, there were little pools no bigger than the lids of tin cans and drops of rain. In those midnight movies there was always a hero, but it wasn't Darvis, not at ten years old, not that day. He shut his eyes. He was in a slow-moving brook that trickled to the Count, unable to resist the shuffle he was in until the end. This was how it always ended if he was able to stay awake on Friday night, it wouldn't take long before the creatures and castles turned into sleep. The TV light would continue to pearl until his mother turned it off and staggered him to bed.

Darvis got his autographed photo that day. It was one of those things he lost a long time ago. But Count Misfit lived on. He remained the same. How could he? How old was he? Every Friday night after the news and the reruns, he would reappear and just like a long time ago Darvis would be covered in a blanket on the couch and the movie that came on would overpower him and become a dream. While the people he knew grew older and some died or began to die, the night told him why.

"Where are we?" Ms. Meredith asked him.

"We're here," Darvis said.

"Where's here?"

"You're at home."

"I'm tired," she sighed. "I don't know why there's a cow."

"I know," said Darvis. "It's a mystery." She couldn't take care of it. She needed Phinneas and Tuesday to take care of her. "I'll go find this Ewell Clagg." Darvis stood and pushed his chair back. Out of the window, he caught a glimpse of Phinneas and Lincoln standing beside the cow, still as statues. A light rain was falling on the green pond.

15.

The SONG

So what did he do? Plying the city streets looking for a man who didn't want to be found, Darvis parked the car beside a phonebooth and got out. It wasn't raining badly, less than a sprinkle really. Lincoln watched him from the car, under a roof behind a windshield that barely let on it was raining. The telephone booth smudged, that's all. Behind that smear was a café.

Darvis stepped inside the booth and lifted the phonebook. It hung on a taut metal coil. There was just enough room on the silver shelf to set the paper book down so he could leaf through it. The pages were feathery soft. A bird could make a nest of them, lining the twigs circled on top of a telephone pole with all the names and addresses in the city. Darvis had a flock to alphabet through.

Nostradamus, Edward, 1127 Walnut Avenue

Nostradamus, Sarah Jane, 853 Key Street

Nostradamus Car Wash, and then Darvis read it aloud, "Nostradamus Investment Corporation." He committed the address to memory. He could do that. A child could do that, turn it into a little song, a Mother Goose rhyme. He was pleased. He left the soft, thick book open on the shelf in case someone else was troubled by cows. Ewell Clagg might be placing them all over town, wherever there was a spot of grass to crop. Clagg's truck held a never-ending supply, soon you couldn't cross a parking lot without running into a cow.

Darvis exited the booth. He imagined a dairy herd crowded on the pavement watching him. Ewell Clagg had to be stopped before that happened. Darvis ran that address song through his head. It was imprinted in there, pressed like the wax groove on a record. He felt good. He took a step towards the car. Lincoln was watching him. The glass was steamed with breath. Then Darvis turned for the café instead. The morning was running away from him, he missed breakfast, he was hungry. Some toast would hit the spot. He could get it to go, with a coffee in a paper cup.

Lincoln looked around the cloud on the glass and saw Darvis go into the café without him.

The door opened and shut. Darvis ordered at the counter. The cook in the kitchen moved back and forth at the stove. Music played. Some young people, boys and girls, laughed with the waitress. It was a nice morning out for them, they didn't have a cow on the loose. And what if they did? Darvis imagined them taking turns, walking it from yard to yard, feeding it neighborhood flowers and grass they pulled from vacant lots. They would have a ball with it. When his toast arrived, he put it on a napkin and spread it with blackberry jam. Lincoln would get the crusts. A few quiet Oldsmobile minutes later, the café door opened. Darvis waved at the car. Lincoln was ghostly in it.

Darvis wiped the window when he got behind the wheel. He had his toast and Lincoln crunched his share and when there was nothing left in the paper cup but a black drop, Darvis fit the key in the ignition. He tried to remember the song he was singing but it was gone. He had to go outside to look at the phonebook again. The song would come back to him the way a radio remembers what it played yesterday.

16.
GARY COOPER

Ghosts were in the window and hanging from the eaves and one on a branch in the tree. There was also a pumpkin. That's what reminded Darvis it was almost Halloween—two more weeks—not Doomsday. Gold letters were painted on the glass door: NOSTRADAMUS I. C.

Darvis let himself in, a bell jangled, a man sitting at a desk looked up from a book. "Good morning!" He gave a jack o' lantern grin. His teeth were stained from cigarettes. One of them smoldered on the ashtray near his hand.

"Are you Mr. Clagg?"

"That's me. 24-7. How are you?" He set his book down.

"Not so good," Darvis answered. "My friend, Ms. Meredith says you left a cow on her property." Darvis glimpsed the book title, *Farming Cattle: From Cow to Carton*.

"Oh yes, a very fine Holstein. And that's only the beginning of Nostradamus Dairy. I can't wait! Fresh milk right here in the city. In fact, I intend to devote all my time to that venture. It's what I've always wanted to do."

"I don't think so. You're not welcome on that land."

Clagg laughed, "What is this, a range war? Are you trying to scare me off? Where's Gene Autry?" He took a drag off the cigarette. "Let me tell you, old timer, I don't scare easy."

"Ms. Meredith didn't agree to this."

"Of course she did! I've got her signature on the deed." He pointed at the file cabinet behind him, the open drawer on top.

"She didn't know what you were doing. She doesn't have all her senses."

Clagg shook his head, "No, she's fine."

"She thought you were the phone company. Is that what you told her?"

"Listen, I came to her with a legitimate proposition and she agreed. I've done nothing wrong. This is how business is conducted."

"You hoodwinked her. She isn't capable of making decisions."

"She isn't? She's lucky to have me as a partner. Do you know what a gallon of milk costs at the store? It's outrageous! We can cut that in half when we sell our own milk. Maybe we'll get a milk truck and sell door-to-door like the old days. Don't you worry about Merriweather, she knows more than you think."

"Meredith," Darvis said. "Her name's Meredith. She can't take care of a cow. That's ridiculous. We don't want your dairy. We don't want your investment plans. Go back to Ms. Meredith and get your cow. End of story."

Tall as Gary Cooper, Darvis turned and left the office, leaving the sound of the bell and a ghost flapping on the door. "So long, Clagg," he could have said before the bright Technicolor sunlight burst over him on his way to his horse.

It was drizzling outside. Lincoln was waiting for him in the car. If it was Gary Cooper on this sidewalk, he would be smiling just a little bit.

17.

GOLD

At the Nostradamus office a daydream formed. It floated over an office desk.

He remembered Dawn. They must have been in grade school when she told Ewell, "I heard about your pet cow" and he was so excited she spoke to him, the next thing he knew he invited her to his house to see it. After she said yes, he realized he didn't have one. What could he do? The same thing he would always do when he was in trouble, he made a call. He telephoned his chauffeur Mr. Jersey and told him to get a cow. How hard could it be? Jersey said fine, "Let me see what I can do, Master Clagg." Clagg was lucky there was always someone like Jersey to rescue him.

After school, her mom drove her up the driveway in a Datsun station wagon, rattling in park as Dawn got out and stood next to the rhododendron. The light on her stayed in his memory, it actually became a real thing, the way gold will stay grown in the earth as long as nobody steals it.

Ewell brought her around the house, following the tire tracks left by the Holler Farm truck. The tracks were fresh, pressed into the lawn. Jersey arranged it. The truck would be back in an hour. Ewell had just enough time to pretend the rented cow was his pet. He could make up stories. Jersey watched them from a distance and waited. The cow was roped to a tree and didn't mind their attention. In the driveway, the girl's mother sat in her car smoking. The radio was on. It was her daughter's station. When a good song came on, they would both sing along.

The cow was always like that, frozen like a scene in a dream in the late afternoon sunshine.

Dawn's family tried to make a living farming in the valley. At some point it didn't work anymore and they had to move. Ewell could have hired a detective to find her, but he didn't. Other things came and went. She faded from sight. Reality becomes a memory and eventually nothing at all. When he thought of her from time to time, he remembered her where that pasture used to be when they were kids, the apple trees and crops, before the rich brown soil was stamped into lots for houses. He couldn't have predicted that.

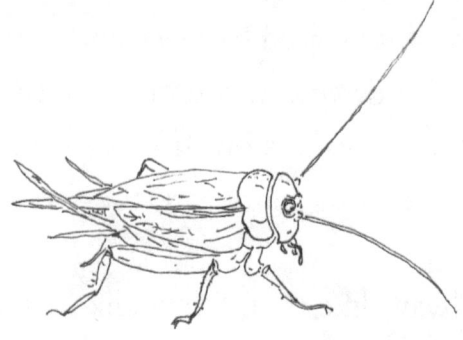

the morning's excitement

18.
STARS

Ms. Meredith was in her room asleep. The morning's excitement wore her out. Tuesday greeted Darvis at the door and they went out on the porch because Tuesday didn't want to be overheard.

"She's getting worse," Tuesday said. And it was happening fast.

It's that cow, Darvis thought as he listened to Tuesday. Ewell Clagg got to her. Darvis couldn't help it—he thought of vampires again. You couldn't stop them, only delay them for a while, nobody could hold onto their life forever.

In the field below, the cow was being a cow.

Darvis told Tuesday about Nostradamus Investment Corporation. He didn't tell her he thought Clagg was a vampire, he said Clagg had a deed with Ms. Meredith's signature, that was all it took to own her and turn her field into a crowded herd.

"No," Tuesday said, "he can't do that."

"That's what I said. But apparently she agreed to let this land become Nostradamus Dairy."

They watched the cow for a minute. It was pleasant to watch, like a giraffe at the zoo, but they didn't know anything about caring for cows. And the thought that there would be more on the way...

"Well," Tuesday said, "We'll have to stop him somehow."

He nodded defiantly.

The wind blew the tall dry grass.

They were stars in a John Ford movie now.

Yes, Darvis left the farmhouse in care of Tuesday waving from the porch, and he steered out onto the winding road headed back to town. But unlike a celluloid cowboy, he didn't know what he was going to do.

A nice view of the bay spread between the trees. No whitecaps today, it was calm as a chalkboard. Gray sky, gray water, a boat going somewhere. Good thing Darvis was driving slowly, a young man stood with his arm held over the road. A hitchhiker.

Darvis eased the car onto the shoulder and waited. It would have been a good plot for a vampire, one who hitchhikes, but Darvis wasn't thinking that—the further he got from Ms. Meredith's trouble, the more the world welcomed him. He swung the passenger door open and greeted the stranger. "Need a lift?"

"Do you know where Lexington Brown lives?"

"The inventor?"

The boy nodded.

"Sure, I know him. His place isn't far from here. I can take you, hop in." Lincoln made room, moving to the backseat.

Olson Redding was his name. He was a poet from Santa Rosa, California. Darvis asked if he came all the way here just to see Lexington Brown and was surprised to hear the answer, yes. The renown of this one man who lived a quiet life in a house on Clover Avenue meandered like a salmon stream all the way down the coast. Olson left the sunshine and followed Interstate-5 north, almost to the end of the line, Canada.

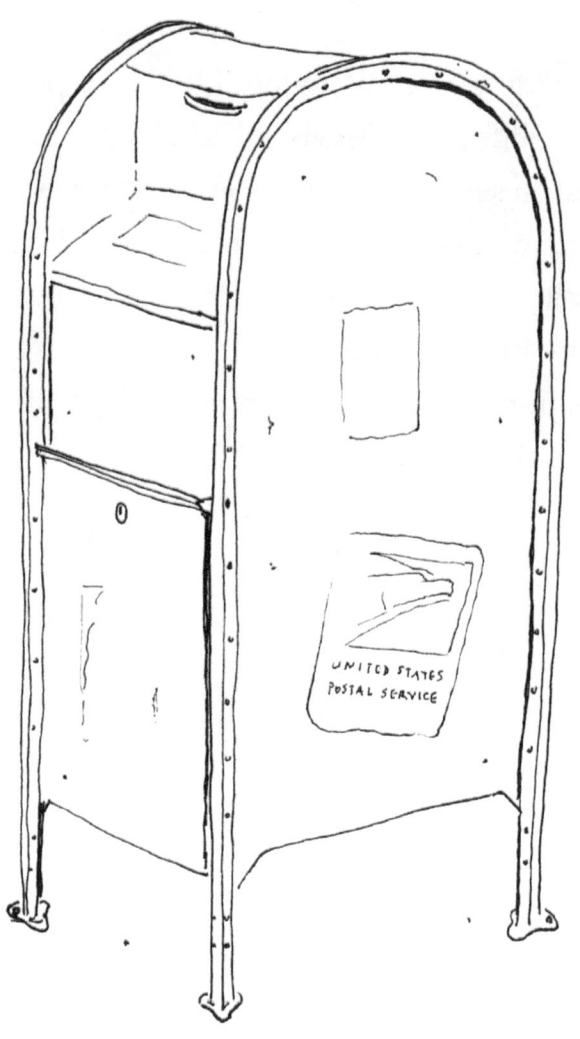

chipping away

19.
LEXINGTON BROWN IS NOT AROUND

13 Clover Avenue was a mailbox beside a driveway. Darvis braked and turned the wheel. The grass was tall enough to fold against the chassis, a whispery sound like seaweed under a hull. Red and yellow trees on either side, orange and brown leaves on the ground.

"There's his house," Darvis pointed, "and there's the garage where he keeps all his inventions." Darvis parked next to an old truck.

Olson regarded it with awe. "That's the Jim McBrady." He didn't need to decipher the painted name rusting and chipping away on the door. "It runs on radio waves."

"Basketball games, to be precise."

"Right. How does it do that?"

Darvis shrugged. "He can make energy out of anything. I don't know."[1]

They left their car. Darvis held the door open for Lincoln. Fall was all around them except for one tree.

---

1 See *Lexington Brown and the Pond Projector*

It was a bright green magnolia flowering next to the porch. Darvis laughed, "Look at that tree! It still thinks it's spring."

Birds were singing on its branches, it sounded like a sunny June afternoon.

Darvis held his hands open to the tree the way you'd greet a campfire. "The air is warm."

Another cold bird swooped in. Word was getting around. They were living in some sort of dream.

"He did this," Olson said.

"I guess so." Darvis should visit more often. Places like this were like fresh springs. "Let's see if he's here."

"Okay."

The ground was soggy. Mindful of their footprints, they tried to avoid the mud on the way to the porch.

Wouldn't you expect Lexington Brown to have something fantastic to announce you're at the door? A mechanical cat to meow a doorbell. It didn't work that way. Darvis knocked on wood. He tried again. Nothing.

A mechanized cat was such a good idea—wouldn't it be great? It could climb the wisteria arch up to the second floor, to tap on the window where Lexington Brown might be napping. Confusing dreams with reality.

Darvis said, "Doesn't seem to be here." He followed the floorboard to the edge of the porch and leaned over the railing. A view of the backyard. A pond with a plank dipping into it. Drooping cattails. A rowboat set to drift, filled with a layer of green water. "Maybe he's in the garage."

Lincoln was fine standing inside the warm circle pouring off the magnolia.

On the other side of Jim McBrady, the garage was anchored in the ruins of summer flowers.

They stopped at a window to look inside. The glass was cobwebbed over. No lights on to see Lexington Brown or the cluttered rows of all his marvelous inventions.

20.
OLSON REDDING'S BOOK

A year later, *The Lexington Brown Collection* was published. Every page was a poem for an invention Olson Redding saw that autumn day. Lexington led him through the garage and up the stairs to the loft and all over the property too, wherever a creation creaked in the rain.

That wasn't the only book Lexington Brown inspired. Picture all the ships lost at sea, the wrecks that litter the silt a mile deep. Crawl with those strange creatures, wriggling eels and sharks, as they go in and out of portholes. Find the cargo hold. Luminous fish slowly bobble. A wooden crate in a stack of barnacle debris. That's how hard it is to find *Lexington Brown and the Pond Projector*. Who knows, maybe a lucky fishing line will catch one. Sure. That could happen someday.

Olson's book didn't have to rely on a deep-sea recovery. His book was carried in shops, displayed in windows, carried on buses, shelved in cafés. He was on the radio and reading in theaters and auditoriums. Hollywood called with a movie deal. He went from hitchhiking to the back of a limo carrying him to *The Sylvan Moore Show*. He never expected his life to change so much with a visit to 13 Clover Avenue. Meeting Lexington Brown that day had been a new invention—a book—and the start of clicking gears and an energy that swept Olson Redding into the air and onto the map.

Darvis never expected that to happen either. "Good luck," he said when he left the boy on the porch, waiting for Lexington Brown to return. The bright green tree plugged into the ground glowed with white flowers. After a year, in the late-night glow of his room—yes, that was still his habit, but he wasn't alone anymore—Darvis would be surprised by the poetry on TV. In a way he helped it to happen. Sylvan Moore blew a smoke ring and asked how the book came to be.

That's in the future though. This book is still in October, four days from Halloween. There's a cow in Ms. Meredith's field. It couldn't be ignored. Darvis and Tuesday cleared a space in the car garage, lay hay on the floor and brought in a heater to keep the place warm. It was an odd sight to see a cow next to an Oldsmobile while the rain fell on the roof and the gray windows looked out on falling leaves. On a stool next to the stall gate was a library book thick as a Bible: *A Guide to Having a Cow.*

21.
FLOWERS

It's funny how buying flowers for someone made him feel so young. There ought to be a label on the cellophane wrapped around the stems: *Caution. This may resemble a romantic act.* Not always of course. Flowers told all kinds of stories. There were flowers for all occasions, but when you saw Darvis leaving Shop N Save with a bouquet of daisies held like a porcelain doll and a smile that couldn't quite hide itself as he glanced at the patchy blue sky on his path to the car, it could be safely inferred he was on his way to Deena.

He was thinking there ought to be more flowers in grocery stores, they ought to be considered a staple right up there with bread and butter. The soup aisle should be followed by a row full of roses and other blooms packaged for any budget. While we're at it, he thought, this is fantasy, why not make them free? They grow all over the city, they ought to be. Flowers can speak without the need for words. If it's hard to say them, Aisle 7 is waiting to help.

Darvis was the only one walking to a car with flowers, there was a daydream America in his mind. What would it take to make it real? He set the flowers on the rooftop while he unlocked the door. What if he got in, started the car, and forgot the flowers up there? And as he slowly drove across the parking lot to the road, waited for a bus and some cars and turned and began to pick up speed, the daisies would lose their hold and start to slide. When they fell off, it would be a whole other fate for them. There's always someone waiting for flowers.

He didn't forget them though. When he sat in the car he put them on the dashboard so they reflected on the window and it looked like he and Lincoln were headed into a garden. The ghostly image overlaid the traffic, the buildings, the posts and wires and sky. Slowing and stopping and carrying on, Darvis was driving a bee following the flowers.

Past the church on the corner, a street, then another, he turned onto hers. The daisies slid on the dashboard. Great yellow trees reached overhead. A couple blocks more and he was there. As he parked he thought he might see her in the window like a fortuneteller with a feeling he was near. But he would find she wasn't at home. He would hold the flowers and knock on her door. It was a good thing he didn't know where she was. It would have worried him right back to Transylvania.

22.
SUNSET DRIVE

It was only a casual belief in vampires now. Why shouldn't it be? They were the stars of dreams and movies, nothing more. He had a lot more on his mind. There was no reason to think Deena was in danger. He just guessed she was somewhere else.

He found a dish of rainwater and propped the flowers in it beside her door. She would know it was his hello. With just the city in his window, Darvis drove back home.

For a moment he thought she might be there. Wouldn't that be funny if Deena had the same idea as him? Or what if she just missed him? What if she left flowers by *his* door? They could go back and forth the rest of the day until they finally met up at the Shop N Save, reaching for the last bunch of carnations. Old movie gray and silver light while Frank Capra swept petals on the floor.

No sign of Deena by the door, no flowers, but when he went inside there was a message on the answering machine. He pressed the flashing red button and listened.

It was Deena, her voice anyway, spindling on the cassette tape recording. She was at the hospital, she was alright, she said she sprained her arm, that's all. "I just want you to know where I am."

"I'll be home in a bit," Darvis told Lincoln. Back to the car. Some gray birds took off from the curb. He hurried but you had to be careful, the sidewalks got slippery after rain. Moss grew on just about everything. His car roof wore a green crown.

Deena at the hospital…He didn't want to think of her there, he didn't like that place at all. How many vampires would be lurking around? He took the freeway to the Sunset Drive exit. It wasn't a long drive but he felt like he was fighting every light to get there. Visitor Parking next right. Painted white lines on the pavement, each one big enough to fit one car. Every space held a car or truck. He drove down two rows before he found a place. It was too bad Lexington Brown didn't invent a car that carries its own parking spot.

The hospital sprawled on top of the rise with cars parked around it. Ominous clouds. It looked like a scene in a Count Misfit movie where our hero has to go into the castle to save the girl. Darvis hoped she was still in there, in one of those hundred rooms. He asked at the reception desk and they said they would check. There was a little bouquet of orange and yellow flowers on the desk. He wished he brought Deena some. There just wasn't time.

23.
DETAILS

Tomorrow was Halloween. Was their plan still going to happen? Deena said, "Yes!" and wagged her elbow done up in a cast. One arm would be enough, she promised. After all, it was her plan. When she heard about Nostradamus Investment Corporation and their only hold on Ms. Meredith was a contract kept in an unlocked file cabinet, her eyes brightened with the idea. They just had to get into the agency. It was lunacy, but Darvis agreed. He would follow her to the moon. They just needed to iron out a few of the details...a big one was calling Lexington Brown to see if he had an invention they could borrow. There had to be something in that garage.

Darvis wanted to make sure Deena was cared for before he left. He made her a can of soup, his specialty he said, and he made a blanket nest around her on the couch. She waved her other arm, "I'm not helpless, Darvis."

"I know." She wasn't a bird with a broken wing. He couldn't think of a world without her. They were paired, she would do the same for him, they took care of each other. He stayed as long as he could until he remembered Lincoln would be wondering where he was.

"Thank you, Darvis," she said. She held a hand up to him and pulled him close. "I feel better now."

"Me too. That was scary." He pointed at the phone on the coffee table. "Call me if you need anything at all."

"I will."

"Day or night."

She smiled. "I promise, Darvis."

"I'll check with Lexington and see if he has an electric lockpicking robot."

"Alright," she laughed. She pictured it.

It was a longshot. Lexington's inventions never seemed to cross that line into nefarious, but Darvis was in luck. Once he got home and dialed 13 Clover Avenue and explained the situation, Lexington told him he had just the thing for the job. Ms. Meredith was his friend too, that library of hers was like a second home to anyone who wanted to make sense of the world.

"Thank you so much," Darvis said. "I'll see you tomorrow."

What a comfort to know the old inventor was on their side.

trick-or-treaters

24.
HALLOWEEN

Ms. Meredith sat in a rocking chair and stared. Something was wrong. "Why is there a cow out there?"

Tuesday could be a tape recorder for all the times she answered that question. The words could be stamped on a penny. The coins were dropped all around the house.

Ewell Clagg was running the figures on an adding machine. He was in the red. Maybe cows didn't pay off until you had a herd of them. The *Herald* sports page was folded open on his desk. He sighed. His old cricket team was on a winning streak.

Deena was reading a book. A record was playing something soft. On her arm, on the cast, the message from Darvis was a drawing of a daisy.

And where was Darvis at this moment? Driving away from Lexington Brown's.

The sun was getting low. The sidewalks on South Hill were hopping with creatures, the trick-or-treaters were already out. Darvis rolled down the window so he could hear the sound.

Halloween was open like a magic door. "Look over there!" he said.

"Is that a robot?" said the strange passenger in the backseat. "Made of cardboard?"

"Sure. This is the night all the ordinary masks come off and people turn into someone else. Look at that giant yellow bird!"

Lincoln was looking back and forth too. A ghost and a cowboy, a girl with a trombone, an astronaut and a cat.

"Isn't it great?" Darvis grinned.

"It's most remarkable," said Lexington Brown's invention.

Darvis stopped the car for a horse costume. Two people inside, two different pairs of shoes. Darvis thought of the cow on the hill in the stall eating hay. If this plan worked, Ms. Meredith would be free of Nostradamus Dairy.

The voice in the backseat said, "I wouldn't mind getting out right here and climbing up in that tree so I could sit on a branch and watch everyone go by."

"Well, if we can get this job done quick I'll drive you back and let you out for the night."

"That would be marvelous."

"Okay," Darvis laughed. This was probably the one time of the year that invention would fit right in. People expected to be scared. "We're almost to Deena's place.

She's the brains of this operation."

"I see…" There was a pause in the back of the car as the street rolled along, the houses, the trees, and the view of the bay. "So what does that make me?"

"You're the muscle," Darvis answered. "You're the hired Robert Ryan-type who steps in and gets the job done."

That must have been a good answer.

Darvis felt like a midnight movie when Sterling Hayden is on the way to one last bank heist. Then, when it's done, he can save the family farm and live his life in sunshine.

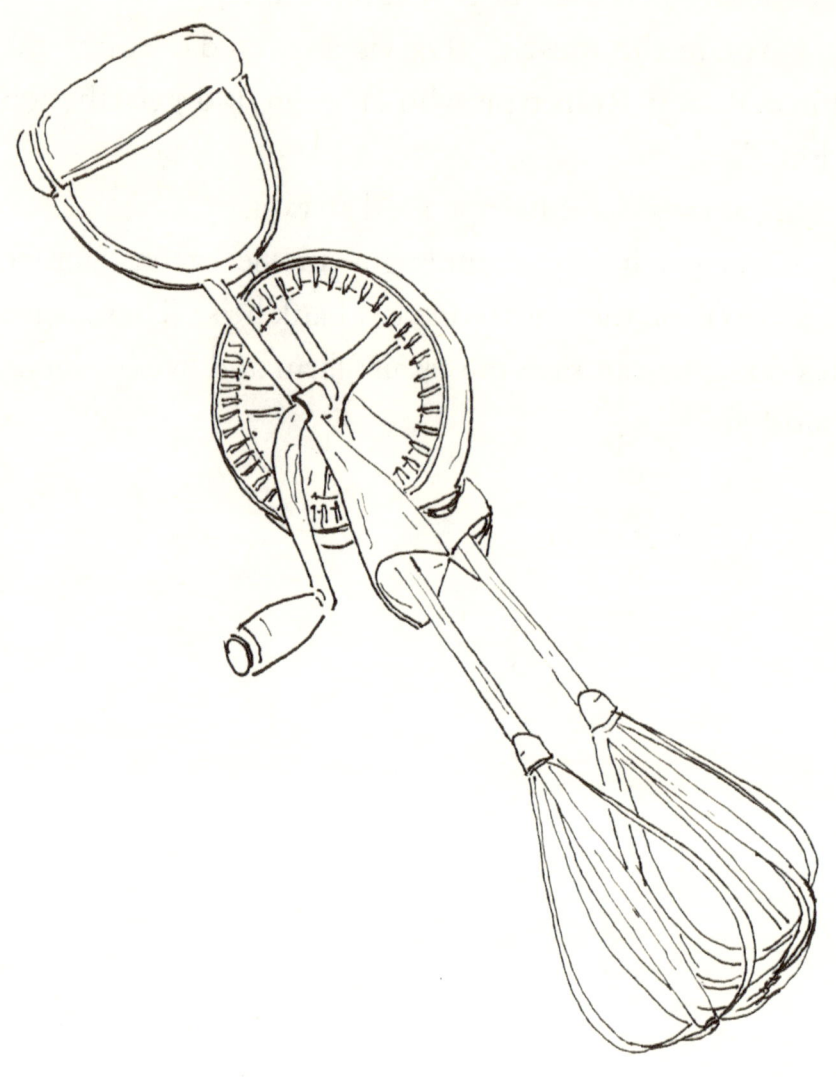

devoted

25.
LEGS O'TOOLE

Legs O'Toole took a little getting used to. He also took up most of the backseat. Darvis, Lincoln, and Deena were pressed along the front bench seat.

"I like your hat," Deena said.

Legs tipped his green and yellow cap. "Tacoma Tigers. Mr. Brown is a fan. He likes teams that don't exist anymore. Strange, wouldn't you say?"

Nobody answered. It was no stranger than a big metal spider in a baseball cap.

Darvis pictured Legs O'Toole in a uniform on the mound, pitching sliders and fastballs, but that wasn't the game tonight. They were only minutes away from Nostradamus Investment Corporation.

The road took them past the orange glows of pumpkins in windows and by doors. Farm trucks brought them into town from the countryside. Whole fields were devoted to growing crowds of them. And now they were hollowed out and filled with candlelight and given a thousand different faces.

"That's a great costume," Darvis told Deena. She was all in black, a black knit hat and a black mask that went just around her eyes. Whiskers were painted on her cheeks. "A cat burglar."

"And what are you tonight, Mr. Darvis?"

"I'm just the one behind the wheel, the one who drives headlong into danger, and the one who takes us out again."

"And the one who forgot to dress for Halloween," she added.

He nodded. "That too." The car slowed and turned. "This is the street."

Deena rubbed her black mittens together. "I'm a little bit scared."

Darvis steered them into the alley and said, "Well I don't think you need to worry, you've got nine lives." He switched the headlights off and the car lumbered along the gloom between the backs of buildings. Garbage cans, potholes, a silver creek of rainwater. A crow took flight in front of them. Darvis laughed, "I thought that was a bat!"

"It sure is spooky," Deena said. "I don't see any numbers or signs, do you know where we're going?"

"Yep. Right here." Darvis pulled the car in tightly next to a brick wall and stopped. "I'll get out your way, Deena. You stay here, Lincoln. Guard the car. This shouldn't take long."

Deena stepped out of the car right into a puddle. "Ugh! Watch where you walk."

Legs O'Toole scrabbled outside and pointed two arms at the wall. "Is that the place?"

Darvis said, "Yes. You think you can pick the lock?"

"I've never met one I couldn't," Legs replied. It only took a second to reach the door and eight arms waved and seized it in the next blur.

Deena shivered. She whispered, "Lexington Brown really outdid himself with that invention." She held her cat's tail from dragging.

Darvis was about to say something but was interrupted by the door snapping open.

"Presto!" said Legs. "Who wants to lead the way?"

26.
LURKNG

Nostradamus Investment Corporation was one office room. It smelled like burnt coffee and cigarettes. "Oh darn," said Darvis, "I forgot a flashlight."

Legs O'Toole responded with a beam of light that fanned across the worn carpeting like high beams.

A crooked painting of a horse tilted on the wall. The desk where Ewell Clagg spent his days was littered with papers, green file folders, and a cup of shadow. A black telephone too, one that hunted out victims and schemes was dormant for now.

Legs swiveled the spotlight until it stopped on the file cabinet hunched against the opposite wall like a pickpocket lurking in a police lineup.

"There it is," Darvis said. They trooped over to it and Darvis pulled the top drawer open. Deena peered over his shoulder. You would have expected the drawer of a five-foot-tall cabinet in an investment firm to be chockfull of clients in vertical folders. Not this one.

Clagg made it easy for them. There was a jar of Sanka instant coffee, a spoon, and a stapled contract.

The light moved as Legs O'Toole ascended the wall and shined down into the drawer.

"That's it," Deena breathed.

They could read Ms. Meredith's name scrawled on the top line. Darvis turned the pages to the last sheet where her signature wobbled at the end.

"We got it," Deena whispered. Her cat whiskers curved around a smile. "Let's get it out of here."

Darvis said, "No, we're not thieves. I have another idea." He handed the contract to Legs O'Toole who took it and crawled back to the floor. Darvis and Deena were silhouettes looking down.

The big metal spider reached into a cupboard that opened on its abdomen.

"What's he doing?"

Darvis said, "You'll see. Lexington Brown thought of everything."

The spider found what it was looking for. Legs turned to face the wall and held the paper flat against it and simply erased the signature with a fine paintbrush. Ms. Meredith vanished from the contract as easy as that. Legs held it in the spotlight for their scrutiny.

It was a work of art.

Darvis chuckled and returned it to Legs O'Toole. "Nice job." Tomorrow that cow was as good as gone.

under a tree

27.
TRICK-OR-TREATERS

On South Hill, Darvis parked under a tree. Legs O'Toole crawled out the window and up into the branches. That was where he wanted to be, his reward. He wanted to watch Halloween flow around him like a river. For a little while, Darvis and Deena and Lincoln did too. It was like a night tide parade. A leaf would fall on the windshield every now and then telling them the spider was still up above.

"We did it," Deena said. "I can't believe it."

Darvis gave her hand a squeeze. "Ewell Clagg is going to be awful surprised when he looks at that contract. I'll give him a call tomorrow and tell him to collect the cow."

"Where did he get a cow anyway?"

"I don't know. A farm somewhere. I hope he kept the receipt."

Lincoln stared at a kid-sized raccoon crossing the street, holding her mother's hand, a bag of candy in the other paw.

Costumes flowed by on the sidewalk. A few more leaves fell on the glass. The nights were getting cold, Deena was glad to have Darvis close.

"It's like a movie, isn't it?" Darvis said and he thought of the pond projector Lexington Brown invented. The whole town was supposed to see their movies underwater.

"It's better than a movie," Deena said.

A gorilla walked past the car pushing a stroller.

Darvis didn't think twice about a Count Misfit floating cape-like wings. That vampire was followed by an alligator and a scarecrow. The houselights shined in the windows along the street. The doors were popping open and closed, laughing and chants of trick-or-treat. In between the branches overhead were moonlit clouds. Halloween had its own sound, like recess at a haunted house.

Twenty feet above the street. Legs O'Toole could have built a web out of kite string and sat in it all night. Lexington's barn-like garage was full of plenty strange creations but nothing like him. Like Frankenstein locked in a castle, how could he never have known about Halloween? He would have liked to stay as long as it took the night to become quiet and calm but he knew he had to return home so he could tell everyone what he saw only a mile from Clover Avenue.

There were less trick-or-treaters. The smaller ones were gone. Legs climbed down from his perch.

A dark leaf twirled and stuck to the windscreen, then

there was a thump on the car roof and eight scratching feet. Legs crawled in the open window.

First, he had to thank Darvis for bringing him here, then he described what it was like watching Halloween from a tree.

If he climbed a little higher and used his telescopic eye pointed east, he could have seen the field on the hill and Ms. Meredith's houselights small as stars.

Darvis started the car. Off they went. Bat wings fluttered in the red brake lights.

this would help

28.
HOLLER FARM

Darvis was pleased to see the end of this adventure wrapping up with the start of the day. The dew on the meadow sparked with the gentle electricity of an uncloudy sky. A beautiful November morning, the sort to write haikus about, cold but alive. Their breath hung in the air like ghosts.

A trailer truck was backing up to the garage. Holler Farm was painted on the green siding.

"What's it doing here?" asked Ms. Meredith.

"They're taking the cow away," Darvis said.

"What cow?"

"The one in your garage."

She was somewhere else, a ghostship had most of her on board. What was left in this world was a frail body. Darvis wished he could go into that foggy world and save her, bring her back. He hoped this would help.

She watched as the truck came to a stop, then said, "There's a cow in my garage?" She seemed surprised but not alarmed. She didn't know what was happening anymore, but there were people around her who were helping. She was going somewhere too. She just didn't know where. Her eyes remained calm. They looked worn as beach stones.

Phinneas barked.

The trailer stopped. The brake lights flashed once before the truck engine died. A burly round man hopped from the cab. He worked for Holler Farm. He knew a cow in the city wouldn't work. He was doing his job, moving quickly to the end of the trailer to fumble with the chain and the ramp.

From the passenger side of the truck, Ewell Clagg emerged. What a lot of trouble he caused. He held a coffee cup and a manilla folder. He wasn't fond of the mud, he picked up each tasseled shoe step carefully. "Well…" he said. He turned his back on Darvis, Deena, Tuesday, and Ms. Meredith so he could take a last look at the meadow. The pond was winter blue. "I guess the world wasn't ready for Nostradamus Dairy." He sipped his coffee. "Not yet." Even with the sun on his gray suit, he still looked like cement. "I'll tell you what though—I don't know how it happened." He turned and waved the folder at them. The trailer ramp clanged down on the ground. "I seem to recall this was a legitimate document signed by Ms. Merriweather. I'd sure like to know where her signature went." Another sip of coffee, "Yes sir, it's a genuine mystery."

Darvis felt Deena's hand tighten on his. They thought they knew what happened but they only knew half the story.

It happened last night in the shadowy office when Legs held the contract, after he erased Ms. Meredith.

"What's your friend's name?" Legs said. "The quiet one we left in the car."

"Lincoln," Darvis told the robot.

Legs made a clicking sound. Neither Darvis nor Deena saw what the robot did next. It was dark and it was sleight-of-hand and he had eight of them to keep track of. With his back to the audience, Legs returned the contract to the file cabinet, put it in and shut the drawer.

ghost

29.
LANTERN

"Don't you think I would have noticed this before?" Clagg held out the contract so they could read it. On the signature line was another name:

Abraham Lincoln

Darvis and Deena were truly surprised.

"What do you make of that?"

"I don't know," Darvis said.

"Yeah," Clagg grunted, "Me neither." He shoved the folder under his arm. "Awful convenient for you folks, though. What did you do, hire Abe's ghost to break into my office and do that?"

They were quiet. It could have been true.

"Anyway, the signature looks legitimate. Maybe I can get something for it."

The truck driver interrupted them, "Where's the cow?"

"Oh—in here." Darvis led everyone to the garage. He and Deena opened the door.

All the clutter you'd expect to see, along with a couple bales of hay, a sack of feed, and a makeshift corral with a black-and-white cow.

"There she is," Clagg said, "My hopes and dreams."

The driver handed him a pink receipt, "Sign this," and fumbled with the rope knot on the gate. This was no place for a cow. He took more time to untie than it should have. The cow shuffled. He almost had the knot undone. He was used to cows. He patted her back. He remembered the Hollers used to have a pet cow. When it was a calf, one of the girls brought it inside the house to live. He used to see it looking out the window when he got to work at dawn.

"Sorry about that knot," Darvis said. "I was never in the Navy or anything like that."

The farmer gave a last tug and the strands fell apart. "Let's get you out of there," he told the cow. "Nice and easy." He squeezed himself into the pen.

"Why is there a cow in here?" Ms. Meredith wondered.

"There won't be anymore," Tuesday said. "He's taking her back to the farm."

"Who is he?" Ms. Meredith's world had returned to a childlike question for everything.

While Tuesday explained, Darvis pressed himself

against the garage support post to make room for the cow. The driver was used to leading cows, but not when they were in garages. And the cow—maybe to show her disdain for the place—kicked her back leg. The big hoof missed Darvis but squarely connected with the wooden post. A lantern on a peg above Darvis's head swung and fell.

Darvis didn't know what hit him. He wouldn't know anything but darkness until his eyes opened again.

repeated

30.
HOSPITAL

"Do you know why you're here?"

Where was here? On Earth, or somewhere else?

The question was repeated.

Do you know why you're here? What a thing to ask. Of course Darvis knew. He wanted to say it's obvious. We're only here for a short while. Ask a flower about that.

There were daisies by his bed.

The room made sense now. Darvis was in a hospital room. The nurse was asking him that question. "Yes," he said and when he saw Deena he said, "Hi. Hi Deena. Are you alright?"

"Of course, Darvis."

A machine steadily beeped.

"Brrr," he said. "It's cold in here."

"I'll get you a blanket," the nurse said and left the room.

Deena quickly moved to his side and held his hand.

"Oh, I'm so happy you're alright. The doctor said you'd be fine to go home tomorrow. Your hands are freezing, dear." She clasped hers around them.

"Is Lincoln alright?"

"Yes. He's at my house. He's fine. Does your head hurt?"

"I don't know," he shrugged and smiled and closed his eyes. "I'm floating along. A beautiful river. You're with me. Thank you."

She leaned down and he could feel her breathing. They were in a hospital but they were also on that river. The water flowed slowly and carried them under green leaves, past a sunny meadow where Ms. Meredith's cow watched them float by.

The nurse tapped twice on the door and entered. The river was gone, the meadow and the sunshine and the cow. "I brought you a blanket," she said.

Deena thanked her. Darvis woke up as she tucked it around him.

"I was asleep," he said. "I'm so tired."

"Yes dear. You should sleep."

The nurse dimmed the light. The machine beeped and a blue dial drew a steady heartbeat.

"You can see me in the morning," Deena said. She whispered, "I'll bring you some strawberry shortcake."

"Yes please…" He couldn't keep his eyes open. He went back to the river and waited for her.

He sat on the embankment and watched the water. A

warm day. The current was green as the sea. A salmon broke the surface. On the other side there were trees and fields and distant mountains.

Behind him were more of those fields, an apple orchard, a few black-and-white cows, and what looked like Ms. Meredith's house.

What am I doing here? he wondered.

Sometimes when you're in a dream you realize it, just before you wake up.

31.
An OLD FRIEND

The hospital room was gloomy dark. The shades were drawn but not all the way, revealing a night sky over the big parking lot. Edgar Allan Poe could be sitting in the chair by the window.

What woke up Darvis was the knocking on the door. The handle rattled clumsily.

Darvis said, "Come in."

The handle slowly turned and the door opened with a creak that sounded like a century of rust on the hinges. The door had grown that old. It could have leaned on a cane as it shuffled open.

"Hello Darvis," said the figure in the doorway. Green hospital light haloed him.

Darvis recognized him. He knew him all his life it seemed. Pick a Friday night in 1976 and chances are Darvis was staying up late on the couch, wrapped in blankets, with the TV taking him to a midnight castle.

"Count Misfit?"

"Greetings." The Count sounded just the same as always, when the lightning and thunder and a howling wolf carried his voice through the air.

Darvis repeated, "Count Misfit…" He didn't need to be hypnotized. "Why are you at the hospital?"

With his black cape flowing, the Count seemed to slide across the linoleum floor. He halted at Darvis's bedside. A cold prickling fog descended with a voice that croaked, "I was visiting an old friend. Now I'm visiting another one."

"You have many friends," Darvis said.

"Yes. Yes, I do."

"I saw you when I was a kid. At the grocery store. I got your autograph."

Count Misfit nodded. "I remember."

"Your movies scared me. I believed in them. I could probably blame you for all my nightmares." He stared at the unblinking eyes. "I don't know which place is harder to survive—the dreamworld or this world."

"They're just stories." Count Misfit replied. "Those are just stories we tell in the night."

"They stayed with me," Darvis said. "All this time."

"They float in the night." Like a bat, an ice-cold hand reached towards Darvis's forehead. "You don't have to worry anymore."

It was true.

It was over just like that.

one of the greatest

32.
LUCKILY

So it would seem. But *The Count Misfit Show* always had to contend with commercials. You could never be sure the Creature from the Black Lagoon would reach the water before Otto Kott might appear flogging a two-for-one carpet deal.

The door opened, light from the hallway poured in and Deena stepped into the hospital room. A big shadow stole away from the bed where Darvis lay. The door clicked quietly shut behind her and the room was dark again.

"Are you awake, Darvis?" she whispered. She couldn't wait for the morning. Luckily. She moved towards him carefully. She was carrying a bowl she didn't want to drop. Something sweet. Strawberries on biscuits topped with whipped cream. One of the greatest things on Earth.

DO YOU KNOW WHY YOU'RE HERE?

Writing: September—December 2024
and January 2025

faithful robot

AFTERWORD

In other words, I let this book write itself. I just woke up every morning, went downstairs, went outside and walked around with a notebook and pen and here's what happened this fall and winter.

I thought I was done, my Halloween book about death seemed finished with the arrival of Count Misfit in Chapter 31. Then in the second week of January my computer died. Did I lose everything I wrote, this book plus another novel in production, and the notes for two more? The screen was black.

I've been using the laptop for years. It's helped me create at least thirty books. A longtime faithful robot. After the monitor lid on it broke, I repaired it with duct tape and set the computer in a sturdy wooden frame. This bit of ingenuity earned it a name: The Amish 4000. That mishap should have been a warning though, I should have accepted then that its days were numbered.

Did this book become the laptop's swansong? Did it kill it? It certainly felt that way. You have to be careful what you write. Not only is writing a response to observing the reality around us, it also creates new paths for that reality to follow. Time after time I've seen things I write become true. [For instance Mabel, and in Chapter 12 where I mention a kangaroo—a month after I wrote that, a pet kangaroo got free from a house and was roaming our town!] I knew the dangers of writing this book about dying, but it had a life of its own. Until it didn't.

Staring at that black screen, I knew I had to do something. I was hoping writing this book didn't self-destruct everything. It couldn't be too late. So I went back to my notebook and wrote a new last chapter, one that didn't end with death.

That done, the next day I brought the Amish 4000 to a rocket scientist's brother. I'm serious, his brother designed the eyes on the Mars rover. I thought he'd be surprised by the sight of a computer in a wooden cradle, but he wasn't. Maybe there are more like it? Maybe he's been to barns in rural Pennsylvania where this is a common fix. With practiced ease he was able to retrieve the machine's last words, an electric Ouija board gasp, the Amish 4000's farewell to the world.

from *The Other Laugh* (1999)

Books by Good Deed Rain

Saint Lemonade, Allen Frost, 2014. Two novels illustrated by the author in the manner of the old Big Little Books.

Playground, Allen Frost, 2014. Poems collected from seven years of chapbooks.

Roosevelt, Allen Frost, 2015. A Pacific Northwest novel set in July, 1942, when a boy and a girl search for a missing elephant. Illustrated throughout by Fred Sodt.

5 Novels, Allen Frost, 2015. Novels written over five years, featuring circus giants, clockwork animals, detectives and time travelers.

The Sylvan Moore Show, Allen Frost, 2015. A short story omnibus of 193 stories written over 30 years.

Town in a Cloud, Allen Frost, 2015. A three part book of poetry, written during the Bellingham rainy seasons of fall, winter, and spring.

A Flutter of Birds Passing Through Heaven: A Tribute to Robert Sund, 2016. Edited by Allen Frost and Paul Piper. The story of a legendary Ish River poet & artist.

At the Edge of America, Allen Frost, 2016. Two novels in one book blend time travel in a mythical poetic America.

Lake Erie Submarine, Allen Frost, 2016. A two week vacation in Ohio inspired these poems, illustrated by the author.

and Light, Paul Piper, 2016. Poetry written over three years. Illustrated with watercolors by Penny Piper.

The Book of Ticks, Allen Frost, 2017. A giant collection of 8 mysterious adventures featuring Phil Ticks. Illustrated throughout by Aaron Gunderson.

I Can Only Imagine, Allen Frost, 2017. Five adventures of love and heartbreak dreamed in an imaginary world. Cover & color illustrations by Annabelle Barrett.

The Orphanage of Abandoned Teenagers, Allen Frost, 2017. A fictional guide for teens and their parents. Illustrated by the author.

In the Valley of Mystic Light: An Oral History of the Skagit Valley Arts Scene, 2017. A comprehensive illustrated tribute. Edited by Claire Swedberg & Rita Hupy.

Different Planet, Allen Frost, 2017. Four science fiction adventures: reincarnation, robots, talking animals, outer space and clones. Cover & illustrations by Laura Vasyutynska.

Go with the Flow: A Tribute to Clyde Sanborn, 2018. Edited by Allen Frost. The life and art of a timeless river poet. In beautiful living color!

Homeless Sutra, Allen Frost, 2018. Four stories: Sylvan Moore, a flying monk, a water salesman, and a guardian rabbit.

The Lake Walker, Allen Frost 2018. A little novel set in black and white like one of those old European movies about death and life.

A Hundred Dreams Ago, Allen Frost, 2018. A winter book of poetry and prose. Illustrated by Aaron Gunderson.

Almost Animals, Allen Frost, 2018. A collection of linked stories, thinking about what makes us animals.

The Robotic Age, Allen Frost, 2018. A vaudeville magician and his faithful robot track down ghosts. Illustrated throughout by Aaron Gunderson.

Kennedy, Allen Frost, 2018. This sequel to *Roosevelt* is a coming-of-age fable set during two weeks in 1962 in a mythical Kennedyland. Illustrated throughout by Fred Sodt.

Fable, Allen Frost, 2018. There's something going on in this country and I can best relate it in fable: the parable of the rabbits, a bedtime story, and the diary of our trip to Ohio.

Elbows & Knees: Essays & Plays, Allen Frost, 2018. A thrilling collection of writing about some of my favorite subjects, from B-movies to Brautigan.

The Last Paper Stars, Allen Frost 2019. A trip back in time to the 20 year old mind of Frankenstein, and two other worlds of the future.

Walt Amherst is Awake, Allen Frost, 2019. The dreamlife of an office worker. Illustrated throughout by Aaron Gunderson.

When You Smile You Let in Light, Allen Frost, 2019. An atomic love story written by a 23 year old.

Pinocchio in America, Allen Frost, 2019. After 82 years buried underground, Pinocchio returns to life behind a car repair shop in America.

Taking Her Sides on Immortality, Robert Huff, 2019. The long awaited poetry collection from a local, nationally renowned master of words.

Florida, Allen Frost, 2019. Three days in Florida turned into a book of sunshine inspired stories.

Blue Anthem Wailing, Allen Frost, 2019. My first novel written in college is an apocalyptic, Old Testament race through American shadows while Amelia Earhart flies overhead.

The Welfare Office, Allen Frost, 2019. The animals go in and out of the office, leaving these stories as footprints.

Island Air, Allen Frost, 2019. A detective novel featuring haiku, a lost library book and streetsongs.

Imaginary Someone, Allen Frost, 2020. A fictional memoir featuring 45 years of inspirations and obstacles in the life of a writer.

Violet of the Silent Movies, Allen Frost, 2020. A collection of starry-eyed short story poems, illustrated by the author.

The Tin Can Telephone, Allen Frost, 2020. A childhood memory novel set in 1975 Seattle, illustrated by author like a coloring book.

Heaven Crayon, Allen Frost, 2020. How the author's first book *Ohio Trio* would look if printed as a Big Little Book. Illustrated by the author.

Old Salt, Allen Frost, 2020. Authors of a fake novel get chased by tigers. Illustrations by the author.

A Field of Cabbages, Allen Frost, 2020. The sequel to The Robotic Age finds our heroes in a race against time to save Sunny Jim's ghost. Illustrated by Aaron Gunderson.

River Road, Allen Frost, 2020. A paperboy delivers the news to a ghost town. Illustrated by the author.

The Puttering Marvel, Allen Frost, 2021. Eleven short stories with illustrations by the author.

Something Bright, Allen Frost, 2021. 106 short story poems walking with you from winter into spring. Illustrated by the author.

The Trillium Witch, Allen Frost, 2021. A detective novel about witches in the Pacific Northwest rain. Illustrated by the author.

Cosmonaut, Allen Frost, 2021. Yuri Gagarin stars in this novel that follows his rocket landing in an American town. Midnight jazz, folk music, mystery and sorcery. Illustrated by the author.

Thriftstore Madonna, Allen Frost, 2021. 124 summer story poems. Illustrated by the author.

Half a Giraffe, Allen Frost, 2021. A magical novel about a counterfeiter and his unusual, beloved pet. Illustrated by the author.

Lexington Brown & The Pond Projector, Allen Frost, 2022. An underwater invention takes three friends through time. Illustrated by Aaron Gunderson.

The Robert Huck Museum, Allen Frost, 2022. The artist's life story told in photographs, woodcuts, paintings, prints and drawings.

Mrs. Magnusson & Friends, Allen Frost, 2022. A collection of 13 stories featuring mystery and magic and ginkgo leaves.

Magic Island, Allen Frost, 2022. There's a memory machine in this magic novel that takes us to college.

A Red Leaf Boat, Allen Frost, 2022. Inspired by Japan, this book of 142 poems is the result of walking in autumn.

Forest & Field, Allen Frost, 2022. 117 forest and field recordings made during the summer months, ending with a lullaby.

The Wires and Circuits of Earth, Allen Frost, 2022. 11 stories from a train station pulp magazine.

The Air Over Paris, Allen Frost, 2023. This novel reveals the truth about semi-sentient speedbumps from Mars.

Neptunalia, Allen Frost, 2023. A movie-novel for Neptune, featuring mystery in a Counterfeit Reality machine. Illustrated by Aaron Gunderson.

The Worrys, Allen Frost, 2023. A family of weasels look for a better life and get it. Illustrated by Tai Vugia.

American Mantra, Allen Frost, 2023. The future needs poetry to sleep at night. Only one man and one woman can save the world. Illustrated by Robert Huck.

One Drop in the Milky Way, Allen Frost, 2023. A novel about retiring, with a little help from a skeleton and Abraham Lincoln.

Follow Your Friend, Allen Frost, 2023. A collection of animals from sewn, stapled, and printed books spanning 34 years of writing.

Holograms from Mars, Allen Frost, 2024. Married Martians try to make do on Earth in this illustrated novel.

The Belateds, Allen Frost, 2024. The Belateds came to Seattle in 1964 and left the four chapters in this novel.

Jones Jr., Allen Frost, 2024. If you're a fan of 1970s television detectives, you'll be at home with this yarn.

Flop, Allen Frost, 2024. The B Minus Gallery presents a timeless work of art, while a seal goes out with the tide and pterodactyls spin in the sky.

Goodwin Plenty, Allen Frost, 2025. An illustrated novel about Mars buying backyards. Let's look in on the Plentys and see what happens.

Do You Know Why You're Here?, Allen Frost, 2025. A strawberry novel, Nostradamus plots, vampires vs. flowers, moonbeam Halloween.

Books by Bottom Dog Press

Ohio Trio, Allen Frost, 2001. Three short novels written in magic fields and small towns of Ohio. Reprinted as *Heaven Crayon* in 2020.

Bowl of Water, Allen Frost, 2004. Poetry. From the glass factory to when you wake up.

Another Life, Allen Frost, 2007. Poetry. From the last Ohio morning to the early bird.

Home Recordings, Allen Frost, 2009. Poetry. Dream machinery, filming Caruso, benign time travel.

The Mermaid Translation, Allen Frost, 2010. A bathysphere novel with Philip Marlowe.

Selected Correspondence of Kenneth Patchen, Edited by Larry Smith and Allen Frost, 2012. Amazing artist letters.

The Wonderful Stupid Man, Allen Frost, 2012. Short stories go from Aristotle's first car to the 500 dollar fool.

Your cashier was DELORES
Thank you for letting me serve you!